the Fox Forest BAND

by lisa lindman

illustrations by chandra wheeler

Enjoy!

The Fox Forest Band by Lisa E. Lindman

©2015. Lisa E. Lindman. All Rights Reserved.

ISBN: 978-1-936449-79-8

Library of Congress Control Number: 2015930609

Lindman, Lisa Erin.
  The fox forest band / Lisa E. Lindman ; illustrations by
Chandra Wheeler.
    pages cm
  ISBN: 978-1-936449-79-8 (hardcover)
  ISBN: 978-1-936449-80-4 (pbk.)
  ISBN: 978-1-936449-81-1 (e-book)
  1. Bullying—Fiction. 2. Friendship—Fiction. 3.
Music—Fiction. 4. Magic—Fiction. 5. Picture books for
children.   I. Wheeler, Chandra, ill. II. Title.
PZ7.1.L56 Fo 2015
[Fic]—dc23

                    2015930609

Illustrations: Chandra Wheeler, C Rain Industries

Graphic Design & Interior Layout: Ronda Taylor, www.taylorbydesign.com

Hugo House Publishers, Ltd.
www.HugoHousePublishers.com
Austin, Texas
Denver, Colorado

Dedicated to Joann Jones

You had a way of brightening up a room wherever you went. I hope I can do the same with my stories. Thank you for being my personal cheerleader and the best mom that ever was. Love you always!

Once upon a time, there was a wood.
Old and beautiful this forest stood.
The creatures there were kind and wise
and lived out happy animal lives.

But one dark day a fog rolled in
and smothered out the usual din.

A silence spread throughout the wood
that none of the animals understood.

No hooting owl or gentle breeze—
It filled the squirrel with great unease.

"There's something wrong with this thick fog,"
the mouse said from his mossy log.

"I agree," said the big brown bear,
"I've never felt this kind of scare."

"I have before, but it's been years..."
"Well, go on, hedgehog, we're all ears."

So the hedgehog let his tale unfold
of an evil wizard, his heart ice cold.

He was known to stalk the forest at night
and give the creatures a terrible fright.

His weapon was an enchanted fog
Croaked from the mouth of a slimy frog.

This magic fog had a devious power;
those it touched would stop and cower.

It swirled around throughout the dark,
hunting until it found its mark.

Then slithering slowly into an ear
would whisper the creature's greatest fear.

"Tell me," said the rabbit, looking pale,
"is beating this wizard part of your tale?

The fog's almost on us, we must think fast
to find a way to hurry past."

Just then a nimble fox leaped into sight,
his smile impish, his eyes quite bright.

"I have an idea," he told his friends,
"to bring this problem to an end."

"The fog's evil power to use your fear
only works if you can hear.

We can beat this wizard and take a stand
by forming our very own fox forest band!"

The fox was known for being smart,
so all jumped in to do their part.

The mice formed shakers from nuts and seeds,
kazoos were made from river reeds.

Beavers found drums and fashioned flutes, and
others made guitars, cymbals and lutes.

They were finished by nightfall,
ready to go,
eagerly waiting to start the big show.

The fox yelled wildly into the night,
"Hello, wizard, we're here to fight!

Our music is loud and a bit off key,
but we'll play proudly, just wait and see!"

The band started playing—what a racket it did make!
The music was so loud, the ground even quaked.
There was singing, strumming and humming galore,
dancing and prancing, laughter and more.

The whole forest applauded
when the trees did sway.

Then the big bear roared,
"The fog is slinking away!"

"Play louder!" the fox yelled to his crew
and started a song that everyone knew.

The band jumped in and added their flair—
Then the fog got thinner and turned into air.

"We did it!" cried the bear and lifted the fox above his head.

"Hooray!" the animals all cheered. "No more wizard to dread!"

"For now," said the fox, "Our forest is back,
but that doesn't give us a reason to slack.
We need to show others what we know
in order to beat this evil foe."

Word spread fast and far that day—
they showed the world the spirit of play.

They traveled all over
with laughter and sound
and taught other creatures
to stand their ground.